No Baths at Camp

by Tamar Fox

illustrated by Natalia Vasquez

KAR-BEN
PUBLISHING

For my mother, Beverly Fried Fox. May her memory always be a blessing. - T.F.

To my friends and family. - N.V.

Text copyright ©2013 by Tamar Fox
Illustrations copyright ©2013 by Lerner Publishing Group

KAR-BEN Publishing
A division of Lerner Publishing Group, Inc.
241 First Avenue North
Minneapolis, MN 55401 U.S.A.
800-4KARBEN

Website address: www.karben.com

Library of Congress Cataloging-in-Publication Data

Fox, Tamar, 1957—
    No baths at camp / by Tamar Fox ; illustrated by Natalia Vasquez.
        p.   cm.
    Summary: Hoping to avoid taking a bath, Max tells his mother about camp, where cleanliness comes from swimming and water balloon fights until Friday evening, when each camper takes a shower to prepare for Shabbat.
        ISBN 978–0–7613–8120–4 (lib. bdg. : alk. paper)
        [1. Camps—Fiction. 2. Baths—Fiction. 3. Jews—United States—Fiction. 4. Sabbath—Fiction.] I. Vasquez, Natalia, ill. II. Title.
    PZ7.F83935No 2013
    [E]—dc23   2012009498

Manufactured in the United States of America
1 – DP – 12/31/12

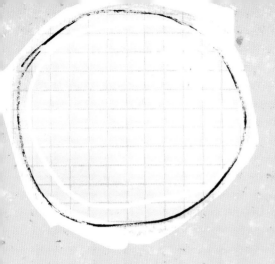
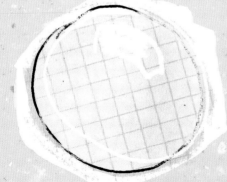

"Bathtime." Max's mother announced after dinner.

"I wish I were back at camp," Max grumbled. "There are **NO BATHS AT CAMP!** No baths for a whole week."

"Really?" asked Max's mother.

"Yes," said Max. "On Sundays we go up the Rock Climbing Wall. We put on harnesses and chalk our hands. When we get to the top, we ring a bell and put our handprints on the wall. Even though we're covered in chalk dust, there are **NO BATHS AT CAMP!**

"On Mondays we have drama. After we paint the sets, we get dressed in costumes and put on make-up. Then we put on a show. Even though we are covered in face paint, there are **NO BATHS AT CAMP!**

"On Tuesdays we help our counselor Yoni build a fire. We gather sticks from the woods and use a magnifying glass to make a spark. Then we roast marshmallows and our hands get all sticky, but there are **NO BATHS AT CAMP!**

"On Wednesdays we go canoeing in the lake. The water is green and muddy and sometimes we catch frogs. Afterwards, we go swimming and my fingers get all wrinkly, but there are **NO BATHS AT CAMP!**

"On Thursdays we go to the art studio. Some of us make bowls out of clay and some of us paint on outdoor easels. We get clay and paint all over us. When we're done, we have a water balloon fight, but there are **NO BATHS AT CAMP.**

"On Friday mornings, we learn Israeli dances on the big field. Some kids play instruments, and others teach us the steps. We dance barefoot and get our feet all muddy, but there are **NO BATHS AT CAMP!**

"On Friday afternoons we shake the sand out of the blankets in our cabins and sweep the floors. We put away all of the sports equipment and hang up our costumes in the drama closet. We clean out the fire pit and scrub the canoes. We decorate the dining room with our artwork.

"And then, just before sundown, we take turns in the showers. We scrub our faces and behind our ears. We wash our hair. Yoni stands outside the showers and inspects us as we leave.

"And then, quick, quick, quick we put on our nice clothes, comb our hair, and run down to the waterfront, where the whole camp gathers.

"Devorah, the camp director, stands in front and calls out, 'Shabbat Shalom everyone!'

"And we all answer, 'Shabbat Shalom, Devorah!'
The counselors lead us in songs to welcome Shabbat.

"Then we all troop into the dining hall. We light the Shabbat candles. Each week a different cabin leads the blessings for the wine and challah. After a special fancy meal, we sing more songs and tell stories.

"On Saturday we get to sleep late. In the afternoon we go for a nature hike, and Yoni tells us stories about growing up in Israel. When we get back to our cabins we tell jokes and scary stories.

"When it starts to get dark we go back to the waterfront and Devorah holds up a braided candle, and passes around cinnamon sticks for everyone to smell. We are saying goodbye to the sweetness of Shabbat. 'Shavua tov, have a good week,' Devorah wishes us. And we all answer, 'Shavua tov, Devorah!'"

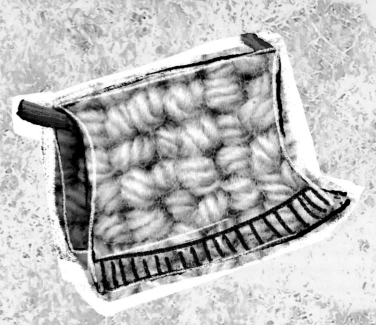

"But Max," his mother said, "We have Shabbat at home. We sing songs and tell stories.

"We take walks around the neighborhood, and at the end of Shabbat I always say, 'Shavua tov, Max!'"

"I know," Max said. "But camp is better because...

There are **NO BATHS AT CAMP!**"

ABOUT THE AUTHOR

Tamar Fox has an M.F.A. from Vanderbilt University and a B.A. from the University of Iowa. Her writing has appeared in *The Washington Post* and *The Jerusalem Post*. She lives and writes in New York and Philadelphia. This is her first children's book.

ABOUT THE ILLUSTRATOR

Natalia Vasquez is a freelance illustrator living in Lima, where she studied painting at the local fine arts school. She works with a variety of media including pencil, ink, watercolor and digital art. She has illustrated both English and Spanish children's books.